Dragon TROUBLE

Sue Cason

Illustrated by Tracie Grimwood

SUPa DOOPERS

sundance

Published by
Sundance Publishing
234 Taylor Street
Littleton, MA 01460

Copyright © text Sue Cason
Copyright © illustrations Tracie Grimwood
Project commissioned and managed by
Lorraine Bambrough-Kelly, The Writer's Style
Designed by Cath Lindsey/design rescue

First published 1998 by
Addison Wesley Longman Australia Pty Limited
95 Coventry Street
South Melbourne 3205 Australia
Exclusive United States Distribution: Sundance Publishing

ISBN 0-7608-3289-7

Printed In Canada

CONTENTS

CHAPTER 1
A Small Dragon

A small dragon fluttered onto a branch. He howled a long and terrible howl that echoed across the land.

Horses tossed their heads. Birds twittered nervously. People put their hands over their ears to block out the awful sound.

A small, howling dragon sets everyone's teeth on edge.

A small, howling dragon keeps everyone from sleeping.

A small, howling dragon must go back into his cage.

As soon as possible.

CHAPTER 2
Princess? What Princess?

King Cyril, Queen Cecilia, and Lester the Jester watched Princess Celeste gallop around the palace grounds on her horse. She whooped and yelled. Her blue eyes sparkled. The wind tugged at her hair.

"Tsk, tsk," said Queen Cecilia. "Celeste, get off that animal at once."

"Yes," said King Cyril. "Come and sit on your throne like a princess should."

King Cyril and Queen Cecilia looked very much like a king and queen. They wore glittering crowns and fine robes, and they carried their scepters proudly. They sat on their gleaming thrones and spoke wisely to their subjects.

CHAPTER 3
Bad News

And the trouble brewed that very afternoon.

King Cyril was reading the royal newspapers.
Queen Cecilia was busy telling Celeste that a
princess should sit *inside* the royal carriage
(not outside chatting with the driver).
Then, into the palace
hurried a man—a weary,
worried-looking man.

"A weary, worried-looking man to see the King and Queen," said Lester loudly.

"King Cyril," said the man, "there is trouble in the land."

"Trouble?" said King Cyril. "What kind of trouble?"

The man trembled. "The worst kind, sire. Dragon trouble."

"Dragon trouble?" asked the King.

"Dragon trouble?" quivered the Queen. "Oh, dear. We haven't had dragon trouble for more than forty years."

"Dragon trouble? What sort of trouble can dragons make?" asked Celeste.

"Princess," said the man, "the dragons are making our lives a misery. They howl all night. They roar and breathe flames. They destroy our crops and frighten our animals. We all have to stay indoors."

The Princess looked at Lester the Jester. "What can we do?"

"Call the Dragonmaster," said King Cyril. "He knows what to do with dragons."

"We haven't seen the Dragonmaster for days and days," said the man. "No one knows where he is. And the dragons are very unsettled, and they're getting unruly. Please help us, sire."

"Lester, fetch my advisors," said King Cyril. "We'll have a plan ready by noon tomorrow."

"Tomorrow?" whispered the man in dismay.

"Tomorrow at noon," said King Cyril.

"Ho, ho," muttered Lester. "I only hope that noon tomorrow is not too late."

Celeste gazed out of the window. "Dragons," she murmured. "I've never seen a dragon."

CHaPTeR 4
The Advisors

Celeste and Lester sat on the window seat listening to the advice of the advisors.

King Cyril and Queen Cecilia and the five advisors sat at a long table.

"Kill the dragons," advised Advisor Number One.

"Yes, chop off their heads," advised Advisor Number Two.

"Impossible," advised Advisor Number Three. "You can't get near enough to a dragon to chop off its head. The flames get in the way."

"People should stay inside their houses until the dragons go away," advised Advisor Number Four.

"Get rid of the Dragonmaster," advised Advisor Number Five. "He isn't doing his job. My brother would make an excellent new Dragonmaster."

"This is very silly advice," said Celeste loudly.

"Shh, Celeste," ordered King Cyril. "Dragon trouble is serious business."

"Put on your crown and robe and find your scepter," ordered Queen Cecilia. "At least try to *look* like a princess."

Frowning, Celeste put on her crown and her robe and found her scepter. But she thought that the advice of the five advisors got sillier and sillier.

"We need to find out what has happened to the Dragonmaster, and what is making the dragons unruly," she whispered to Lester.

"Quite true, Princess," he agreed.

"Then let's go," said Celeste. "We can solve this dragon problem before they sit down to supper."

"Ho, ho," said Lester, as they hurried to the stables. "This could be fun!"

CHAPTER 5
The Dragonmaster

Celeste and Lester rode through the town.
No one was around. Dogs weren't barking.
Birds had stopped singing. In the stables,
horses whinnied and stamped their hooves.

Celeste's crown bounced around on her head as she rode. Her robe flapped behind her. Her scepter got in the way of the reins. She thought about putting them all in her saddlebag, but she remembered what her mother had told her. She should at least look like a princess.

They rode out of the town, past empty fields.

"Where are these dragons?" asked Celeste.

"The Dragonmaster lives on Mist Mountain," said Lester, pointing to a tall peak. "Perhaps we should ask him."

As they started up the winding road, they passed a mill. Its waterwheel was still. The miller had locked the door and was hiding under his bed, in fear of unruly dragons.

A fine mist drifted down from the mountain. The only sound Celeste heard was the horses' puffing and panting.

"Where is this Dragonmaster?" Celeste asked.

"He lives in a hut," said Lester, peering into the mist. "Look, there it is."

Celeste knocked boldly on the door with her scepter. A low moan came from inside. She opened the door.

There, lying on the floor, was a man—an old man with a long beard. He wore a dark tunic and a cap pulled down to his ears. He looked at Celeste and Lester with watery eyes, then groaned softly.

"Dragonmaster, what happened?" gasped Lester, going to his side.

"My small dragon flew out of his cage and onto a rafter," answered the Dragonmaster. "I stood on the stool to get him down, and I fell. I must have hit my head. I remember nothing. Where are my dragons? I can't hear them. Where are they?"

Lester tried to help the Dragonmaster to his feet, but the old man staggered, then fell back to the floor. "My ankle," he wailed, "my ankle!"

Together, Celeste and Lester lifted the Dragonmaster onto his bed.

"Lester, you must fetch the doctor at once," ordered Celeste. "I'll wait with the Dragonmaster."

Lester nodded. "I'll be back before nightfall." He ran to his horse, jumped on, and galloped toward the castle.

CHAPTER 6
Princess Celeste's Task

No sooner had Lester disappeared than Celeste heard a shrill howl that made her skin tingle. "What's that?" she whispered.

"My littlest dragon," said the Dragonmaster. "When he's not in his cage, he gets frightened. He howls and howls and upsets everybody, especially me."

"I'll catch him," said Celeste.

"You?" The Dragonmaster stared at her.

"Tell me what to do, and I'll do it!" she said with a grin.

"If you open the door to his cage," said the Dragonmaster, "he'll fly in at once. Don't be afraid. He won't hurt you. Well, not much, anyway."

"It seems odd that everyone fears one little dragon," said Celeste, picking up the cage.

"Aah," said the Dragonmaster, "it's not the little one people fear. It's the other two— the big ones."

"The big ones?"

Somewhere on the mountain, a grumbling roar grew louder and louder, until even the floor beneath Celeste's feet shook.

"By the sound of that roar," said the Dragonmaster, "one of my big dragons has an aching tooth. It must come out to make way for the new one underneath. Bring him to me. I will knock it out."

A burst of flames lit up the sky for several seconds before disappearing, leaving a fading glow.

"And by the look of those flames, my other big dragon has the hiccups. Without me, he gets terribly confused and forgets how to get home. Bring him to me. I will give him a drop of a special potion to stop the hiccups."

"So all I have to do is bring home three dragons," said Celeste.

The Dragonmaster nodded. "Hanging on the doorknob is a collar and leash. Slip it over the head of the hiccuping dragon, and he will follow you like a lamb."

"Are you sure?" asked Celeste, as the roaring began again.

"As sure as dragon's breath is fiery hot," said the Dragonmaster. "Farewell. And good luck!"

"All right," said Celeste. "I'll see you soon, with all three dragons."

"I hope so, girl," said the Dragonmaster, as the roars of the suffering dragons echoed around the mountain. "I hope so."

CHAPTER 7
The First Dragon

"Now," said Celeste, "where is that dragon with the hiccups?"

She looked down the mountain toward the mill. The dragon was drinking water from the river near the mill to try to stop his hiccups. But one came every twenty seconds, exploding in a burst of flames.

Celeste ran to the mill. "Come on, dragon," she called. "Come home to your master. He will stop your hiccups."

Now, this dragon *was* confused. Who was this girl? Where was his beloved master? He shook his head and bellowed just as he hiccuped again. The flames shot into the sky and set fire to the mill's thatched roof.

Inside the mill, under his bed, the miller smelled something burning.

"Put this on, dear dragon," soothed Celeste, reaching up with the collar, just as the dragon hiccuped again. The collar caught fire, and Celeste dropped it on the ground.

"Oh, dear! Now what shall I do?" she wailed. Just then, her heavy crown slipped down over one eye.

Her crown! Celeste had an idea.

She took off her crown and, before another hiccup came, she slipped it over the dragon's head and tied the leash to it. "Come on, dragon," she said, "come home to your master."

The miller crawled out from under his bed. He looked out his window. The roof was on fire.

The dragon felt a heavy collar around his neck. He looked at the girl who gently tugged on the leash.

"Come on, dragon."

The dragon was about to roar his refusal
when something hit him.

It was the miller's shoe.

The dragon hiccuped loudly, and flames
scorched the grass.

The miller ran off to find a bucket of water.

"Come on, dragon," said the girl, in such a kind voice that the dragon decided following her was not such a bad idea.

They walked to the hut.

There, with his remedy for hiccups, was the dragon's beloved master.

CHAPTER 8
The Second Dragon

Celeste now set out in search of the second dragon.

She found him on a steep ledge, rocking from one foot to another, his large head swaying as he tried to ease the pain of his aching tooth.

"Come on, dragon," Celeste said, "come home to your master."

The dragon looked at her, then bellowed and clawed at his mouth where the aching tooth throbbed. If only his beloved master was here. He could knock out that troublesome tooth in an instant.

R!

Celeste peered into the dragon's open mouth. She saw the tooth, which was quite gray and wobbly. "*I* could knock out that tooth," she said.

The dragon blinked and put his head to one side. Then, as the pain grew, he opened wide his mouth again.

47

Celeste raised her scepter and, quick as a wink, knocked out the fang.

Ker-plunk!

The dragon began to roar, when, from the corner of his eye, he saw his troublesome tooth tumble over the ledge. He turned to gaze at Celeste.

"Is that better?" she asked.

The dragon smiled—a partly toothless
kind of smile—and nodded his large head.

Celeste tucked the scepter in her belt.
"Let's go, then, home to your master."

The dragon flicked his tail and lumbered
down the mountain after her.

CHAPTER 9
The Third Dragon

The third dragon was in the forest, sitting in a tree, wailing and squealing.

Celeste found him easily.

The little dragon knew the sun would soon set, and he would have to spend another night in the dark. He was very tired. He missed his beloved master, who spoke to him kindly and fed him tidbits through the bars of his cage.

o o OOH!

Celeste opened the cage door. "Come dragon, come."

The little dragon clung more tightly to the branch. Who was this girl? And what was she doing with his cage?

Celeste rattled the door, "Come on, dragon."

The little dragon was confused. He didn't know what to do. He looked up at the sky and howled his awful screaming howl.

Celeste put her hands over her ears.

The little dragon kept howling—louder and louder.

Celeste dropped the cage and grabbed for the dragon's leg. She missed.

The dragon fluttered to a higher branch.

She tried again to grab him, but he was out of reach. "How will I catch him?" she muttered. She stepped back, almost tripping on her robe.

Her robe!

59

"The Princess?" said Lester.

"Isn't he beautiful?" said Celeste, as the dragon whose hiccups she had cured, leaned against her.

"The Dragonmaster says he will give me a dragon of my own," said Celeste.

"Ho, ho," said Lester. "What will your mother and father say about that?"

Celeste put on her robe and took her crown from the dragon's neck. "As long as I look like a princess," she said with a grin, "I don't think they'll mind. Do you?"

aBOUT THE aUTHOR

Sue Cason

Sue lives in a small fishing village in Australia, with her fisherman husband, Baz, and her three children.

In her life she has had trouble with cats, dogs, birds, mice, ducks, hens, roosters, geese, tortoises, fish, cows, horses, lizards, snakes, spiders, flies, and occasionally, snails.

Luckily, she has had a really easy time with dragons—so far.

aBOUT THE ILLUSTRATOR

Tracie Grimwood

Tracie Grimwood lives and works near Melbourne, Australia.

Tracie likes to draw pictures and play with her horses. She has a small horse named Ferdinand and a big horse named Willoughby. And now she has a medium-sized horse named Bess. She lives with her best friend, Jamie, and a black dog named Noah.

Tracie has been drawing and coloring for a long time, and she's very good at staying in the lines.